A Box for Ross

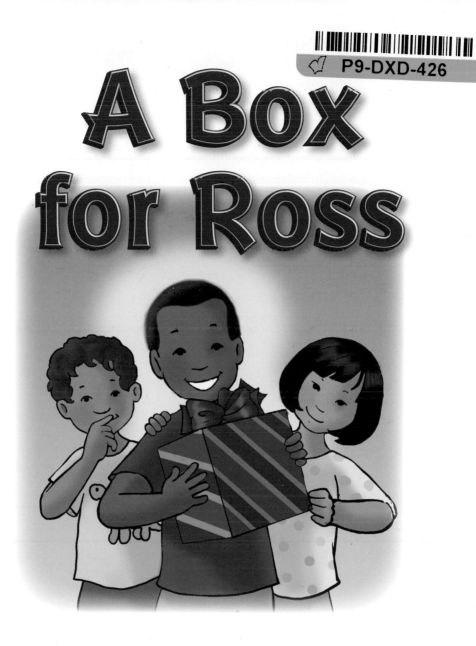

Suzanne I. Barchers

CALGARY PUBLIC LIBRARY

AUG 2019

P9-DXD-426

Consultants

Robert C. Calfee, Ph.D.
Stanford University

P. David Pearson, Ph.D.
University of California, Berkeley

Publishing Credits

Dona Herweck Rice, *Editor-in-Chief*
Lee Aucoin, *Creative Director*
Sharon Coan, M.S.Ed, *Project Manager*
Jamey Acosta, *Editor*
Robin Erickson, *Designer*
Cathie Lowmiller, *Illustrator*
Robin Demougeot, *Associate Art Director*
Heather Marr, *Copy Editor*
Rachelle Cracchiolo, M.S.Ed., *Publisher*

Teacher Created Materials

5301 Oceanus Drive
Huntington Beach, CA 92649-1030
http://www.tcmpub.com
ISBN 978-1-4333-2415-4

© 2012 by Teacher Created Materials, Inc.

Ross got a box.

Ross said, "Look what
I got. I got a box."

"The box has a tag.
The tag says Ross."

Ross said, "I got a
dog? A dog for
Ross?"

San said, "No, Ross.
There is not a dog in
the box."

Ross said, "I got a cot? A cot for Ross?"

Kip said, "No, Ross.
There is not a cot
in the box."

Ross said, "I got a
top? A top for Ross?"

Ren said, "No, Ross.
There is not a top in
the box."

Ross said, "I got a rod?
A rod for Ross?"

Gus said, "There is not a rod, or a dog, or a cot, or a top in the box."

The kids said, "Stop! Look!"

Ross said, "Socks! I got lots of socks in a box!"

Decodable Words

box	in	rod
cot	kids	Ross
dog	Kip	San
got	lots	socks
Gus	not	tag
has	Ren	top

Sight Words

a	or
for	said
I	says
is	stop
look	the
no	there
of	what

Extension Activities

Discussion Questions

- Why do you think Ross gets a box?

- When do you get to unwrap a box?

- Ross asks if he got a dog. Do you think a dog would come wrapped in a box? Why or why not?

Exploring the Story

- Make a list of each item Ross thinks might be in the box: a dog, a cot, a top, and a rod.

  Talk about how each word has the short *o* vowel sound. Replace the *o* in *dog* with the letter *i*. Read the new word. Make as many changes as possible by using the letters *a* and *i*. New words may include *cat*, *dig*, *rad* (slang), *rid*, *tap*, *tip*.

- Place objects in a box that have the short *o* vowel sound. Reach into the box and describe what you feel. Have children guess what object you are touching. Remind children that the word has the short *o* vowel sound. Once they have guessed the word, write it down and discuss how it has the short *o* vowel sound. Let children take turns reaching inside the box and describing the item they touch first.

  Possible items to place in the box include: a toy dog, a toy fox, gong, a toy hog, lock, log, a toy ox, pod, pop, pot, rock, rod, sock, top, wok.